There's No Such Thing As Monsters

by Michael Yu

This book belongs to

_____

The sky has turned purple, the evening has come.
Bedtime is here for everyone.

"But how can I sleep?" says one sleepy head, "with all
of the monsters, under my bed?"

"What's this I see, poking under the bed, long, stringy tentacles, all colored red?

I'm sure it's a monster from down in the deep, coming to stop me from going to sleep."

"Of course not," says Mommy, while reaching down under, then pulling up a red, fluffy jumper.

"It's only your sweater, not a monster at all. Now lay down your head on your pillow so small."

"It's time for sleep; it's time for bed. There's no such thing as monsters; it's all in your head."

"What's that, over there?" young sleepy head says. "There's something blue, there under the shelves.

"It's shiny and flat and slippery too. I'm sure it's a monster, all covered in goo."

"Of course not," says Mommy, while crossing the room,

then reaching in under the shelves in the gloom.

"It's only your truck with its smooth shiny sides. Now

lay down your head, and close your blue eyes."

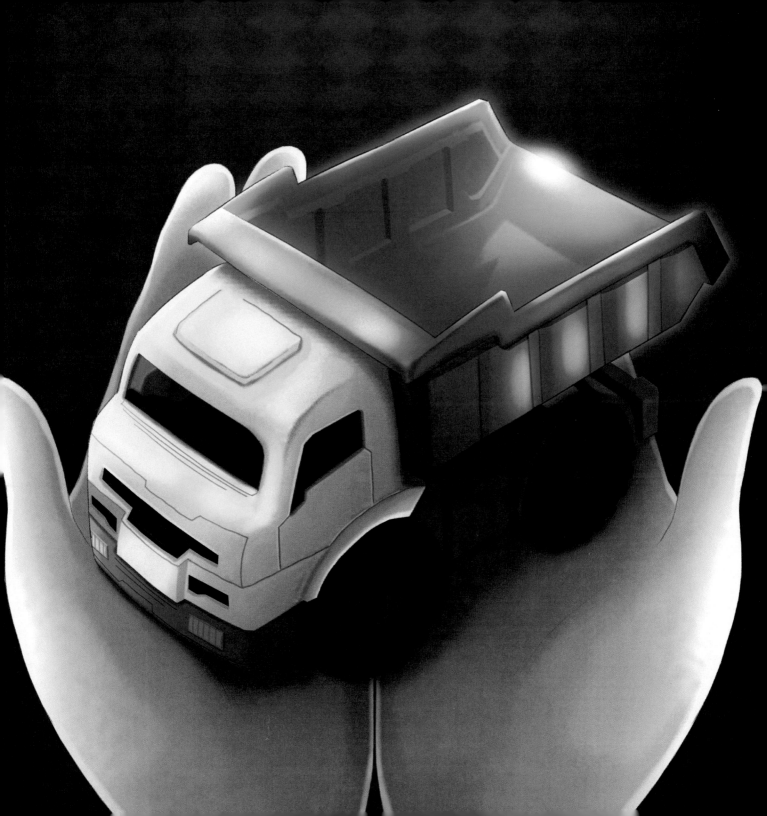

"It's time for sleep; it's time for bed. There's no such thing as monsters; it's all in your head."

"But what's that I see," says sleepy head once more. "There's something creeping out of the closet door.

"It's long and green, with lots of legs. It's coming to eat me! Right here, in my bed!"

"Of course not," says Mommy, who's opening the door, finds a pair of green trousers, lying there on the floor.

"It's just your trousers, lying here by your shoes. Now lay down your head, it's time for a snooze."

"It's time for sleep; it's time for bed. There's no such thing as monsters; it's all in your head."

"But what's that now, Mommy," says sleepy head again. "I'm sure I see something, in the dark over there.

"It's purple and big and ever so fluffy. It's there, by the window, beside my stuffed puppy."

"I'm sure that's a monster, I've seen him before. I think that his house is under the floor."

"Of course not," says Mommy, approaching the window. "Now lay down your head on your soft feather pillow.

"It's time for sleep; it's time for bed. There's no such thing as monsters; it's all in your.....OH!"

But this monster's real, what rotten luck! It's not trousers, or a jumper, or a blue shiny truck!

It's big, purple and fluffy, but what's this I see? This monster is crying. He's as sad as can be.

"What's wrong, purple monster?" asks the sleepy little boy. He'd never seen a monster crying before.

"It's just not fair," the big monster cries. "Children are scared of me, but I'm really quite nice.

"I'm soft, and I'm fluffy, and I'm really no trouble. Just give me a chance, I'm lovely to cuddle."

"My teeth aren't all spiky, and my skin isn't slimy. And just stroke my fur; it's not at all wiry."

"I'll pick up your toys and read stories in bed. I really just want to be your friend.

"We monsters have had a terrible rap. But we're really big softies; we're not at all bad."

And so it was, from that day on, that children and monsters made a break from the norm.

For young sleepy head told all of his friends, "Monsters aren't monstrous; they just want to be friends."

And now, dear reader, it's plain to see. It's bedtime for children like you and like me.

But now, you can see, there's no need to fear the monsters that sometimes at night time appear.

They're just big old softies; they're no harm at all. They just want to be friends with you all.

And even monsters have to go to bed. So good night, little monster, my own sleepy head.....

Made in the USA
Columbia, SC
11 October 2021